PAPER LANTERNS

STEFAN CZERNECKI

Charlesbridge

Published by Charlesbridge
85 Main Street, Watertown, MA 02472
(617) 926-0329
www.charlesbridge.com

LIBRARY OF CONGRESS CATALOGING-IN-PUBLICATION DATA
Czernecki, Stefan.
Paper lanterns/Stefan Czernecki.
p.   cm.
Summary: With the lantern festival close at hand, Old Chen,
the master paper lantern maker, must find an apprentice with
the talent to continue his work.
ISBN 1-57091-410-9 (reinforced for library use)
ISBN 1-57091-411-7 (softcover)
[1. Lanterns—Fiction. 2. Persistence—Fiction.
3. Apprentices—Fiction. 4. China—Fiction.] I. Title.
PZ7.C999   Pap 2000
[E]—dc21   00-057721

Printed in Korea
(hc) 10 9 8 7 6 5 4 3 2
(sc) 10 9 8 7 6 5 4 3 2 1

Illustrations done in gouache on handmade St. Armand paper
Cut-paper lanterns on text pages handmade in China
Display type and text type set in Wonton and Humanist
Color separations by Sung In Printing, South Korea
Printed and bound by Sung In Printing, South Korea
Production supervision by Brian G. Walker
Designed by Diane M. Earley

A note about the Chinese characters:
The two characters that appear on the last
page of the book mean "friendship" when
written together. On the title page, the
characters mean "moon," "happiness,"
"longevity," "wealth," "prosperity," and "sun"
(clockwise from the top right). The two characters
on this page mean "bamboo" when written together.

The author wishes to thank Sun Jie, Cultural
Consul at the Consulate General of the People's
Republic of China in Vancouver, for his careful
review of the text and illustrations. Thanks also
to Heather O'Hagan, Executive Director of
Dr. Sun Yat-Sen Classical Chinese Garden;
Timothy Rhodes; Kurt Strelau; and Ming-Hui Wu.

For Buzz Rhodes
—S. C.

Bamboo strips, sheets of rice paper, paste, and paint were all it took for Old Chen to make the most beautiful lanterns in all of China. But Old Chen was getting tired, and lately there was a stiffness in his hands when he worked. He wondered if the time had come to close the shop. There was no one to replace him, for neither of his apprentices seemed to be blessed with his skill.

One evening a small boy passed by the lantern shop. He stopped to watch as Old Chen carefully arranged the glowing lanterns in the window. It was like seeing a magician light up the night sky with dancing stars. "What a marvelous place," the boy thought. He was filled with curiosity and awe.

When Old Chen looked up, he saw a small, smiling boy standing before him. Old Chen noticed how the boy's eyes lit up as he looked around at all the lanterns. "What is your name, little one?" Old Chen asked.

The boy answered shyly, looking down at the floor. "Little Mouse."

"Ah! Little Mouse. Is that because you are so small?" Old Chen smiled.

Little Mouse looked up at Old Chen and asked boldly, "Can you teach me to be a lantern maker just like you?"

Old Chen laughed and replied, "Perhaps."

From that day on, Little Mouse stopped often at the lantern shop to watch Old Chen work his magic. The two would sit and sip hot tea and eat bowls of steaming rice. Each time Little Mouse would ask to become an apprentice, and each time Old Chen would smile and say, "No, Little Mouse. You are still too small, and besides, I already have two apprentices." But Little Mouse persisted until one day Old Chen said, "All right, Little Mouse, I will give you work. You can sweep the shop for me."

Little Mouse would arrive early in the morning to sweep the floors while the other apprentices performed their duties. He swept around the boy who cut the paper. The apprentice always boasted, "I am the only one who knows how to cut the paper, Little Mouse. You must keep my area clean." All the while he swept, Little Mouse carefully watched everything the paper apprentice did.

He swept around the boy who shaped the bamboo. The boy always boasted, "I am the only one who knows how to shape bamboo, Little Mouse. You must keep my area very clean." Little Mouse nodded and smiled. All the while he swept, he carefully watched everything the bamboo apprentice did.

Little Mouse always swept slowly around Old Chen, watching as the paper and bamboo turned into intricate lanterns in the old man's skilled hands. Little Mouse could not believe that anyone could create such delicate objects. It seemed that Old Chen's hands had magic in them.

Every night Little Mouse would take home used strips of bamboo and old pieces of rice paper to practice what he had seen at the shop. For many weeks he struggled to bend the bamboo into the right shape, just as the bamboo apprentice did. He tried to cut the paper just like the paper apprentice, but he always cut it too small or too big.

Little Mouse had often heard Old Chen counseling his apprentices, saying, "Work slowly and carefully, and you will learn." So Little Mouse crafted lantern after lantern until one night, after pasting perfectly cut paper over a flawless bamboo frame, he took a deep breath and dipped his brush into the paint jar. He labored over the brush strokes until at long last the lantern was complete. He could hardly wait to show it to Old Chen.

The next day, Little Mouse waited until the two apprentices had left before placing the lantern timidly—but proudly—on Old Chen's work table. Old Chen stopped his work and looked sharply at the young boy.

Suddenly, Old Chen broke out laughing, for he knew that at last someone could carry on his work. Little Mouse had the magic in his hands.

The old man was excited now, and he almost forgot about how stiff his hands were. In the weeks that followed, Old Chen told Little Mouse many stories about lanterns and lantern makers. Every evening when the two apprentices left, Old Chen closed the shop and cleared a small space on the table. He sat Little Mouse on a stool beside him and taught him all the secrets he knew about making paper lanterns. Little Mouse listened quietly, watched carefully, and practiced persistently. He quickly learned far more than the two apprentices.

Months passed, and soon the lantern maker and his apprentices were busy preparing for the annual lantern festival. Once all the usual lanterns had been made, Old Chen began planning his masterpiece: a fearsome, majestic dragon.

Shortly before the festival, it began to snow. The snow fell all night, and by morning the streets were cold and covered with a white blanket. When Little Mouse arrived at the shop, he found Old Chen sitting at his table shivering from the cold. His old hands were just too stiff to make another lantern. Old Chen looked at Little Mouse with tired eyes and gently touched the boy's shoulder. "Are you big enough now, Little Mouse? My hands have lost their magic."

"Don't worry," the boy replied. "You have taught me well."

That morning when the two apprentices arrived, they found only Little Mouse sitting at Old Chen's work table.

"Old Chen is not well today," Little Mouse said, "but there is much work to be done."

"But who will make the dragon lantern?" the apprentices asked.

"I only know how to cut paper," the paper apprentice sniffled.

"I only know how to shape bamboo," the bamboo apprentice complained.

"Well, then I suppose I will have to make the lantern," Little Mouse said firmly, and he set to work. He gave paper to the paper apprentice and told him to cut a dragon shape. He showed the bamboo apprentice what shapes to form, and he watched both boys carefully, making sure they made no mistakes. The apprentices were surprised by how much Little Mouse acted and sounded like Old Chen.

Little Mouse's small hands fluttered like butterflies as he repeated what he had seen Old Chen do so often. When the dragon was assembled, the two apprentices could not believe their eyes. It was every bit as beautiful as Old Chen's work.

On the day of the lantern festival, dazzling lanterns in the shapes of rabbits, tigers, fish, horses, and peacocks were carried down the street. The drums and gongs grew louder and firecrackers exploded as a fantastic dragon lantern appeared. Word spread quickly that at last Old Chen had found a master lantern maker to carry on his work.

Old Chen and Little Mouse watched the parade from the window above the shop. The two friends glowed with happiness, just like the paper lanterns.